D0419625

THIS WALKER BOOK BELONGS TO:

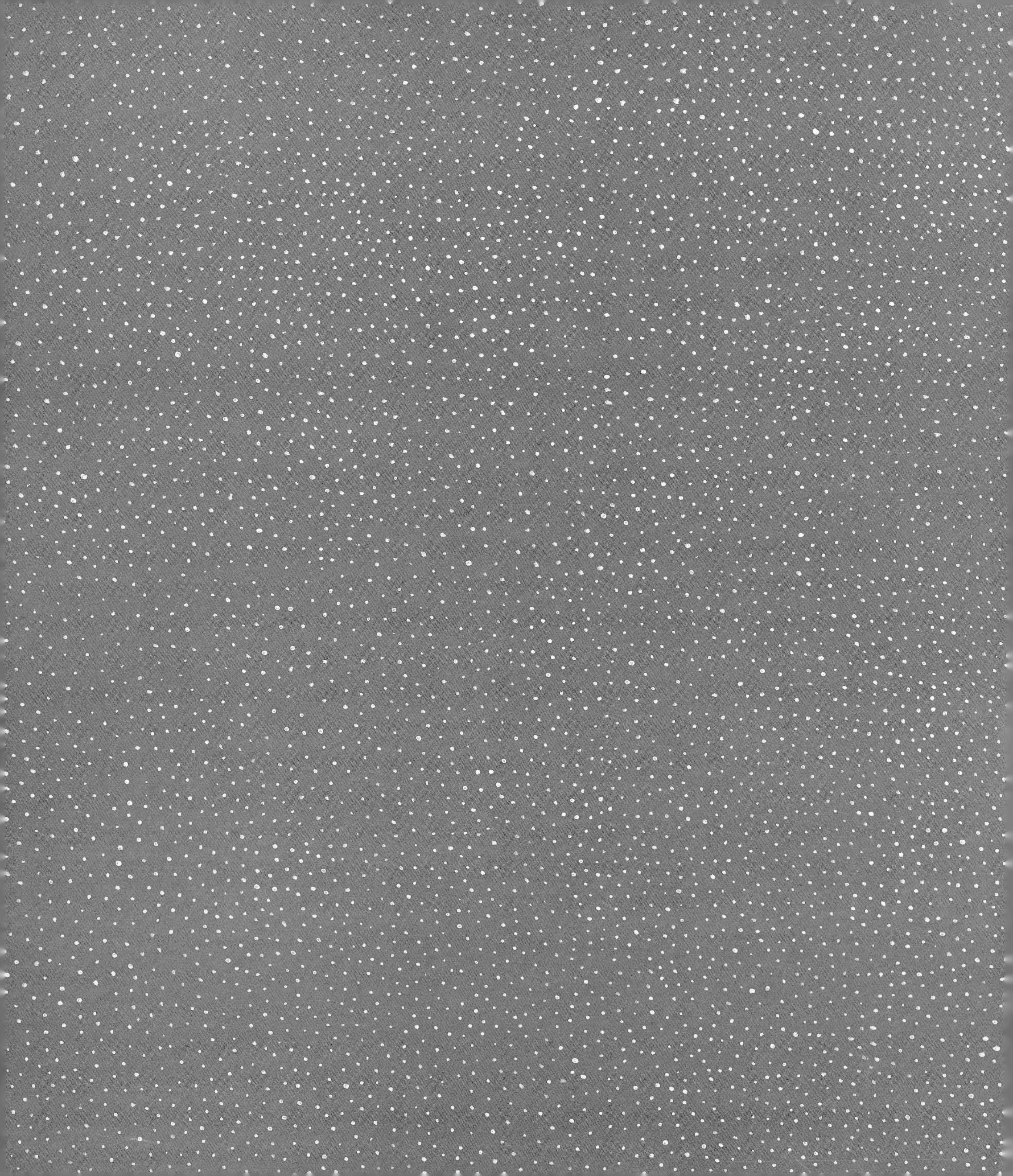

To Martha
K.L.

To Sophie and George, Honeybear,
Snoopy, Theodore, Woolie and Poor Pitiful Pearl
W.A.H.

First published 1998 by Walker Books Ltd
87 Vauxhall Walk, London SE11 5HJ

This edition published 1999

2 4 6 8 10 9 7 5 3

Text © 1998 Kathryn Lasky
Illustrations © 1998 Wendy Anderson Halperin

This book has been typeset in Monotype Columbus.

Printed in Hong Kong

British Library Cataloguing in Publication Data
A catalogue record for this book is
available from the British Library.

ISBN 0-7445-6961-3

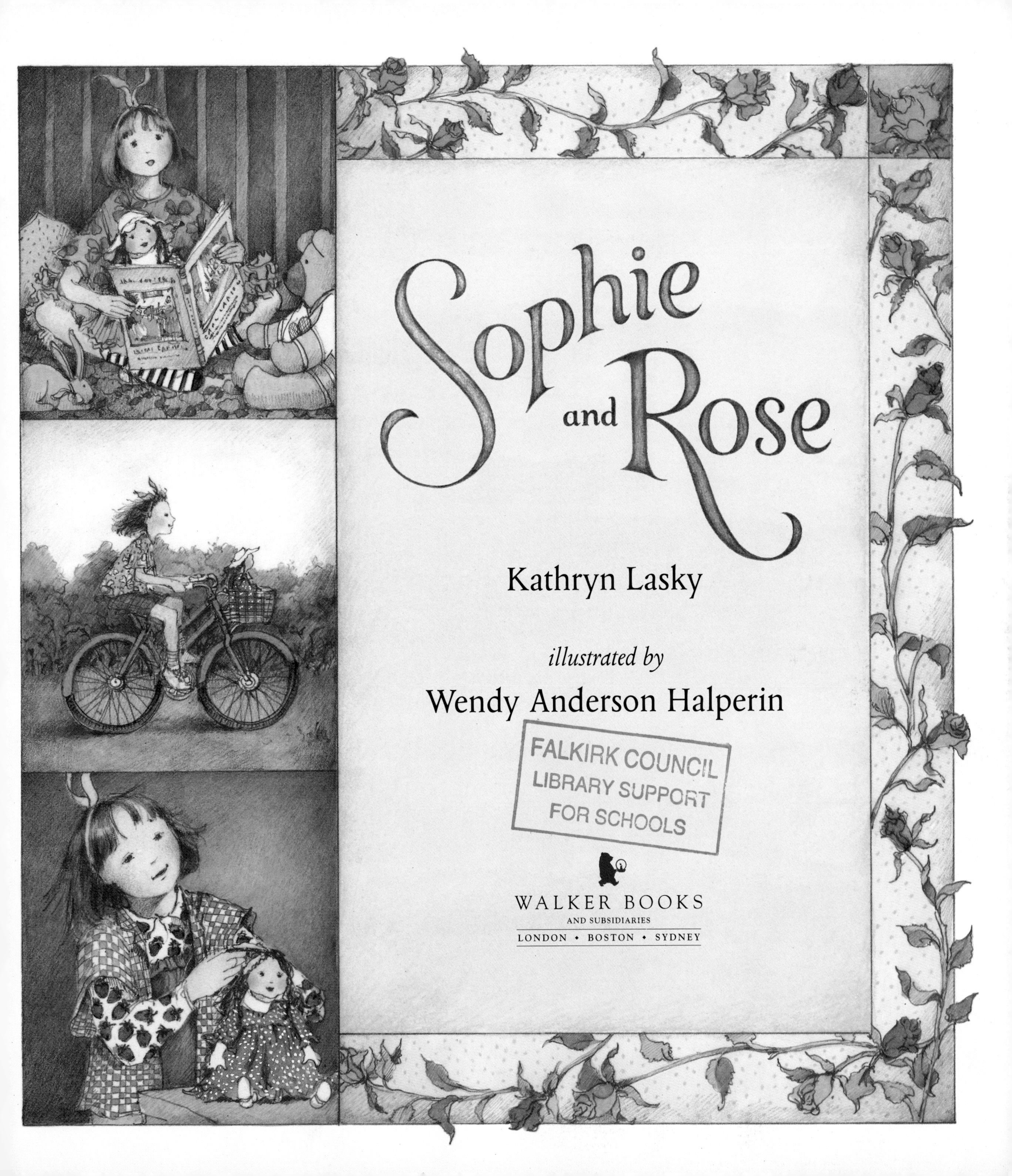

Sophie and Rose

Kathryn Lasky

illustrated by

Wendy Anderson Halperin

FALKIRK COUNCIL
LIBRARY SUPPORT
FOR SCHOOLS

WALKER BOOKS
AND SUBSIDIARIES
LONDON • BOSTON • SYDNEY

This is Sophie's doll.

She belonged
to Sophie's mother when
she was a little girl and before that
she belonged to Sophie's grandmother.
The doll was so old-fashioned that
she seemed like a visitor from another time.

When Sophie
found her, she was wearing a
thin dress with a shredded hem. Her
cheeks were faded and had tiny crackles,
and her mouth was a dingy pink. But Sophie
loved her all the same, and she named her Rose.

In Rose's hair
there were knots that had
tangled up years and years ago.
Sophie wanted to comb them out, but she
yanked a little too hard. A bit of Rose's hair
came out, leaving a small bald patch.

So Sophie took a
little bunch of Rose's hair and
parted it gently. Then she made two
skinny little plaits as thin as crickets' legs.
She promised Rose she would try to be more
careful when she played with her.

But a few days later,
Rose fell and chipped her nose.
Sophie had been playing with her bear
family and had perched Rose on the windowsill
next to them. The chip was tiny, but Sophie
felt terrible. The bears would have bounced without
a bruise to their furry faces and button eyes.
But Rose – well, Sophie saw that Rose was different.

She was old, and really
much more fragile than a stuffed
bear. Sophie decided that the window seat
and not the windowsill was a safe place for Rose.
So she tucked her in all comfy with pillows and
an old blanket. Sometimes at night the moon shone
on both their faces. "Moon friend," Sophie whispered,
and she thought she saw Rose's faded face grow brighter.

For a while nothing bad happened to Rose. Then one morning, Sophie saw something soft and fuzzy bubbling out of Rose's arm. The old stitches in the seam just above Rose's elbow had given way, and the stuffing had begun to pop out.

Sophie's mum
stuffed it back in and stitched
Rose up tight with brand-new thread.
Sophie put her in a box lined with cotton
and tucked her in with the old blanket and
read a book to her. Rose soon recovered.

Usually Sophie
played with Rose in the house.
But once when she was camping in
the garden with her best friend, she got
lonely for Rose and brought her outside. Sophie
and her friend ate chocolate and biscuits and drank
orange juice as they waited for darkness to fall.

Sophie cuddled Rose
tight all through the night. But in
the morning, she discovered that she had
rolled over on Rose and Rose had rolled over on
the last bit of chocolate. It had squished into the
tiny crackles of her cheek. So now Rose had a little
stain, but she smelled so sweet when Sophie kissed her.

One time
something much worse
happened – Sophie forgot Rose.
They had been playing and she accidentally
left Rose just off the path, by the stone wall
where the hollyhocks grew.

In the morning
when Sophie remembered and
came back for her, Rose was lying on the
grass and had only one eye. But that one eye
was still blue-grey, the same colour as Sophie's,
and Rose was still the same old Rose.

Sophie tried
to imagine what Rose
had seen that night in the garden.
A spider spinning a web in the tall grass?
A bat swooping through the sky?
A firefly growing dim at the edge of dawn?

Did she see
how the crickets shape
their songs with their wings or
how the dew drops form and turn the
night lawn silver in the moonlight?
Sophie looked and looked for Rose's other eye.

But a few days later
it started to rain, and it rained
and rained and rained. Sophie knew then
that the eye had washed away for ever. She kept
Rose very close to her and told her how sorry she
was about her eye, about leaving her in the garden.

She told Rose how
brave she was and said that she,
Sophie, could never spend the night alone,
all by herself outside. She whispered this in Rose's
ear. Sophie was sure that Rose could hear in her own
special way. Her ears reminded Sophie of tiny seashells.

Dolls don't
grow up, or grow old.
They grow softer. And the more
Sophie played with Rose the softer she grew.
After Rose lost her eye, Sophie began to take
her to bed every night. And if their faces were

very close together
as they slept, Rose's face would
turn damp from Sophie's breathing.
Soon Rose was very squooshy and so cuddly.
Sophie could bunch her up and tuck her close
while she slept, and feel Rose's soft shape all night long.

Morning
and evening, winter and
summer, Sophie and Rose were
always together. On rainy days Sophie
took Rose to the attic to cuddle, and
sometimes they played hide-and-seek.

Once it took
Sophie a long time to
find Rose. She looked for her
everywhere between stacks of boxes,
behind a shelf of old toys, in shadowy
corners strung with cobwebs.

At last Sophie
found Rose in a trunk filled
with old clothes. There she was,
floating on a silky sea of Spanish shawls,
her feet in a tangle of pearls, her head on

an Eskimo moccasin,
and a bride's veil over her face.
Sophie wondered what Rose thought
had happened. Had she gone to Spain or
Alaska, become a bride or an Eskimo princess?

Sometimes
Sophie still wonders where
Rose's other eye might be. But she
has grown used to Rose with her one eye
and her chipped nose and her new stitching
and her plaits like crickets' legs.

FALKIRK COUNCIL
LIBRARY SUPPORT
FOR SCHOOLS

She knows she
will always love her Rose,
who listens with her seashell ears,
who still smells of chocolate,
and who was so brave through the
long garden night.

MORE WALKER PAPERBACKS

For You to Enjoy

THE HIDDEN HOUSE

by Martin Waddell / Angela Barrett

Winner of the WH Smith Illustration Award

The classic tale of three wooden dolls and the changing fortunes of the house in which they live.

"An atmospheric fable… The mystery in the text is enhanced by fine, evocative illustrations."
The Independent

0-7445-1797-4 £4.99

MY FRIEND HARRY

by Kim Lewis

James takes his toy elephant Harry everywhere – around the farm, on holiday, to bed…
Then, one day, James starts school.

"An altogether charming picture book… Bound to be a much-returned-to-favourite with 3–6 year olds." *The Junior Bookshelf*

0-7445-5295-8 £4.99

GORILLA

by Anthony Browne

Winner of the Kate Greenaway Medal and Kurt Maschler Award

When Hannah's father gives her a toy gorilla for her birthday,
it's the beginning of a magical night out.

"Joyous and moving… A tour de force." *The Times Literary Supplement*

0-7445-9997-0 £4.99

Walker Paperbacks are available from most booksellers, or by post from B.B.C.S., P.O. Box 941, Hull, North Humberside HU1 3YQ

24 hour telephone credit card line 01482 224626

To order, send: Title, author, ISBN number and price for each book ordered, your full name and address, cheque or postal order payable to BBCS for the total amount and allow the following for postage and packing:
UK and BFPO: £1.00 for the first book, and 50p for each additional book to a maximum of £3.50.
Overseas and Eire: £2.00 for the first book, £1.00 for the second and 50p for each additional book.

Prices and availability are subject to change without notice.